Big River Rescue

Adapted by Naomi Kleinberg from a script by Bruce Talkington
Illustrated by DRi Artworks
Cover painted by Don Williams

🐝 A GOLDEN BOOK • NEW YORK

Golden Books Publishing Company, Inc., New York, New York 10106

Library of Congress Catalog Card Number: 98-88803 ISBN: 0-307-16261-3 R MCMXCIX

One lovely spring afternoon, Scuffy the Tugboat floated
happily next to the dock on the big river that was his home.
His friend Seamore the Seagull was napping peacefully nearby.
Although the river was full from the spring rains, the water
was calm. It was a great day for a swim.

And in fact, only a little way upriver, Beatrice Beaver was about to take a swimming lesson from her mother. Beatrice was still learning how beavers do things.

"Mama," she asked, "what kind of trees taste the best? Where does the river end? Why don't fish have legs?"

"My, what a lot of questions you ask!" said her mother, smiling. "I'll answer them a bit later. But right now it's time for your swimming lesson. Follow me."

Mama Beaver slid gracefully into the water.

"Wheeee!" Beatrice cried as she followed with a big splash.

"Now, remember not to swim into the middle of the river," her mother cautioned. "The current there is too swift, even for me!"

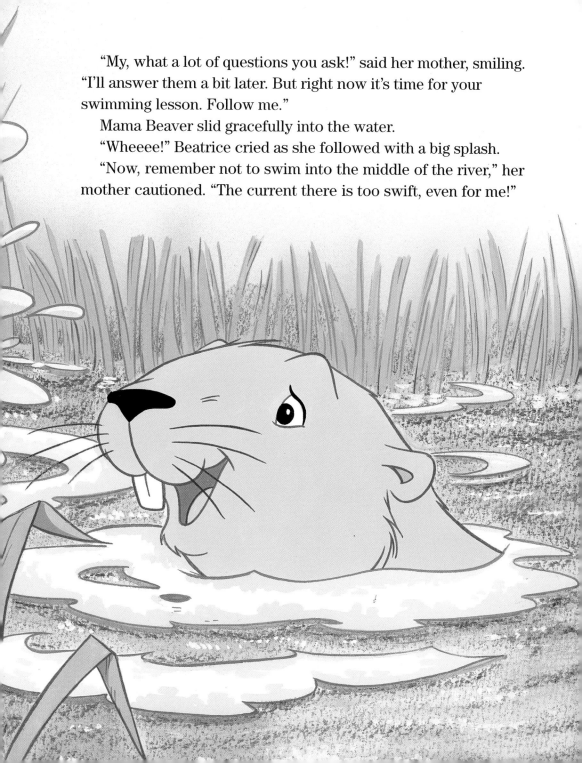

Beatrice ducked into the water and a few minutes later popped up again right next to Scuffy.

"Hey, Scuffy," she called. "Why's that blue tube in the middle of your back?"

Scuffy woke with a start.

"It's . . ." Scuffy began.

"Don't you have any arms?" Beatrice continued. "I've got four feet! You have big eyes just like mine!" She blinked at Scuffy to show him.

"Can you go underwater?" Beatrice went on. "I can! Watch this!"
Once again Beatrice dove under the water.

"Beatrice, stay close," Scuffy warned.

"Is this close enough?" asked Beatrice, giggling as she popped up right behind Scuffy.

Scuffy tooted in surprise. Beatrice gurgled with laughter.

A moment later, Mama Beaver appeared. But Beatrice had
already disappeared again!

"I don't think she's paying attention," Scuffy said.

"When she gets excited she doesn't listen well," Mama
Beaver agreed. "Where is that child? Beatrice?" Mama Beaver
looked around. She was worried.

Suddenly Beatrice emerged again—but this time in the middle of the river, where the current was fast and strong. And no matter how hard she paddled, Scuffy and her mama kept getting farther and farther away.

"Oh, help! Mama, help! I can't get back to shore!" she cried.

Beatrice's mama swam out to get her. But the current was too strong, even for a grown-up beaver. She turned and hurried back toward the dock.

"Scuffy!" she cried. "Please help! I can't get to Beatrice! The current is too strong!"

Scuffy gave two short blasts from his smokestack. "Two toots for an emergency!" he said, summoning Seamore.

"I hear you, Scuffy," Seamore said, taking to the air. "I'll keep an eye on the little one until you catch up!"

In the meantime Beatrice was struggling to keep
her head above water.

"Hurry up—somebody!" she called.

Then, just in time, Seamore arrived. He swooped down, grabbed Beatrice by the scruff of her neck, and lifted her out of the water.

But Beatrice was a heavy little beaver. Seamore had never even tried to carry so much weight before.

"Gee, thanks, Seamore," Beatrice said with relief.

"You're quite welcome, little lady," the bird replied. But he had to open his mouth to speak, and when he did, he let go of Beatrice!

Down she fell—splash—into the river again.

"She's too heavy for me," Seamore called as Scuffy chugged into sight. "We've got to get her in a hurry—she's almost at the rapids!"

Scuffy gave another toot and, with a burst of speed, raced past Seamore. "Hey, Scuffy," Seamore shouted, "wait for me!"

Meanwhile, Beatrice had reached the beginning of the rapids. In this rocky place the water was rough and moved faster than ever.

"Scuffy!" she cried as she made it safely through the rocks, paddling madly with her little beaver feet.

"Mama!" she called again, shooting through another part of the rapids.

Scuffy tried valiantly to catch up with Beatrice, but the current was too fast for him. Still, he didn't give up.

"Whoaaa," Beatrice shouted as she rode the foaming water through a final set of rocks. "Yeeeee-ah!"

Finally Scuffy made it through the rapids, not far behind Beatrice. He spun this way and that in the swirling water. At one point he almost turned over! But he refused to let the rough water get the best of him.

"Hang on, Beatrice," he called. "Help is on the way."

Seamore flew over. "You'd better hurry, Scuffy," he cried. "She's almost reached the waterfall!"

"Oh, no," Beatrice whispered, closing her eyes. "Maybe if I don't look it will go away!"

But then she heard Scuffy chugging up beside her, huffing and puffing. "Climb aboard, Beatrice," he urged. "Hurry!"

With Beatrice safely aboard, Scuffy turned and with all his might tried to head back upstream. But the current was too strong.

"I can help, Scuffy," Beatrice said when she realized what was happening. Using her tail as a paddle, she steered Scuffy away from the really strong current in the middle of the river.

Seamore flew above them. "That's it, you two," he called. "Teamwork really *works*!"

"Can we go home now?" Beatrice asked Scuffy as they headed back to the dock. "I've had enough fun for one day."

"So have I," Scuffy answered.

"I'm sorry I didn't listen to Mama," Beatrice said shyly.

"That's okay, Beatrice," Scuffy assured her. "Sometimes we have to learn from our mistakes."

When they reached the dock, Mama Beaver rushed over to make sure Beatrice was okay.

"Did you thank our friends for rescuing you?" she gently asked her daughter.

"Thank you for being so brave, Seamore," Beatrice said.

Seamore blushed. "Don't mention it, little one," he replied.

"And thank you, Scuffy," Beatrice added, giving him a big hug.

"Oh, that's okay," Scuffy said with a big smile."After all, that's what tugboats are for!"